NOBODY

ILESSIE AND FELICIA WHITE

MILTON & HUGO L.L.C.
4407 Park Ave., Suite 5
Union City, NJ 07087, USA

Website: *www. miltonandhugo.com*
Hotline: *1- 888-778-0033*
Email: *info@miltonandhugo.com*

Ordering Information:
Quantity sales. Special discounts are granted to corporations, associations, and other organizations. For more information on these discounts, please reach out to the publisher using the contact information provided above.

Library of Congress Control Number: 2024902152
ISBN-13:   979-8-89285-021-6   [Paperback Edition]
                 979-8-89285-022-3   [Hardback Edition]
                 979-8-89285-023-0   [Digital Edition]

Rev. date: 09/24/2024

This story like many had to be told about society and particularly about the inner demons of just one city in greater America. As I try to tell my story, it is my hope that I, a mere spectator can articulate the shock of some truths and fictions that will allow the reader to experience the shock and the lines where we ask is it fiction or something our minds won't accept as anything but fictions, but is it really.

Nobody

Taxi hack taxi hack the taxi hack is the non-license drivers who sit on the opposite side of the street calling to customers for a cheap ride were the honest hard working taxi drivers have hustled and pawed out a living on Broad and Susquehanna for decades and the few that remain in the cesspool of life that the infection of drugs and depravation that come with this as many cities throughout the country face the same condition which leads me to our main character which for all purposes we will call Nobody .

But first, let me say because of the identity of some of the people in our little story we must take great care that if there is any such thing as innocence's it can be protected, see because we are all culpable and there are none that are truly innocent...

Society Hill is one of the most prominent areas of Philly connected to Center City Philadelphia also some of the city's most prominent families live and play as most of the city feels the pressure of the changing climate.

Julie Katz, one of those not so Jewish girls coming from a Jewish family in constant confrontation with her family about just wanting to party just like most of the well to do kids of Philly party go to school and just live life in the moment as if life is a forever thing.

The speed line is a subway that gives access to all parts of the city in minutes at very high speeds rumbling through dark and light flashing from points about as darkness flickers from disconnections and in those moments awe, awe as if in a dream of violent fire through the base of the brain and this flash of light and memories in flashes seeming an eternity overcoming the pain penetrating deeply in the base of the neck sharp direct and peace slowly, slowly, some say that in our dying moments our last thought is a cautionary memory from those who love us telling us of our safety of person and our actions.

Last stop, last stop as the engineer comes to the yard knowing as he always knows that the homeless buy one ticket and ride all night and some times in the day particularly at night in the winter as this year is extremely cold he has been on this line half his adult life and to be kind he lets them ride as long as they follow his rules and at least buy one token but there are some simply fall asleep from the warmth of the ride and who is he not to do, as much as possible to help when he can.

This one look as if she has had a bad night he thought the stopping of the train would have awaken her but as he approached her, she seemed to be in an angel like sleep and he hated to do what he had to as he called out to her he got no response, then he knew he had to touch her and he hated that even more these people out here didn't have the means to take care of themselves. As he touched her, trying to shake her awake, he noticed a tiny crimson red about her lips and that she was cold to the touch and as he noticed she was not the usual no smells no raged attire she seemed to be out of place, God she's dead and on my train, looks like my shift isn't over yet, going to have to deal with Philly PD tonight, those assholes...

2:43 AM, Detective J Macfaras didn't relish the idea of being awaken out of his drunken so needed sleep as if this morning was different from all mornings Detective Macfaras had come to the conclusion that his home his career was over and all he had to do was go through the motion having understood that the cities resources were not allocated to crimes in his part of the city,a call from the dispatch in the septa train yard another stiff most likely an OD are a killing involving the killing of the poor and under privileged of the city, he didn't always feel this way but years of death and alcoholism had taken its toll but the truth be told on his worsts days he was a better detective than these new college preppies they were getting on the force just like the rookie detective the captain said was to meet at the crime scene this morning no doubt some one that is supposed to be my new partner sucks...

Nobody

Feel the pain the justice the pleasure they all cheered they all said in a song kill the bitch kill the bitch as if in a song in the head beautiful songs sang over and over in unison each note heightened as threw wool and skin the sharpened steal eased its way to the base of the neck instantly paralyzing then onward to sleep peaceful sleep and an ecstasy like no other, she was ok I liked her more than the others but she just insisted to come here so she could get her stuff to take her reality away.

3:50 PM, as Detective Macfaras makes his way through yellow tape Captain Baldwin and the rookie detective stand talking, Captain Baldwin has seen his better days and I wonder who he pissed off to get the 15th precinct, this no man's land that is all but forgotten.

Macfaras, this is your new partner detective Davis, we won't get into introductions looks like we have a real case finally someone from the DA's office came down. The victim is Julie Katz, family some important people to the city don't fuck this up yea yea...

4:19 AM come with me. I guess we at the hip just make the best of it and don't say anything, moving her head back no obvious wounds but this little prick at the neck she seems to be healthy except that. Detective, bag that little paper sliver over there we want everything...

Davis this your first no. where I'm from North 5th and Girard Ave growing up see a lot of that, but this little girl down here where she has no business going to cause a lot of trouble in the hoods around here. One thing for sure, this wasn't no accident somebody targeted her.

Nobody

They tell me to hurt to destroy and to run they see you no matter where you are. My chest is like fire can't breathe the cold so cold, I just want to rest sleep, sleep, so tired …

Nobody

8:23 AM, Damn, I'm cold got to find my stuff find my stuff, what did I do she didn't deserve that but it's not my fault they keep telling me to they keep making me do as if something or someone else has control of me, I wish it wasn't this way I wish it wasn't, pain in my leg stinging wet with blood I must have fallen on my pick …......

10:00 AM Detective Davis we been filling and at this for hours go home and get some sleep and we meet up at the crime scene about 5 this evening.

Macfaras had one thing on his mind, and it wasn't sleep he needed a drink his nerves were working overtime, who am I to go against the order of things maybe one of these days I'll stop but until then I need a drink,pulling up at the Top Hat the Neighborhood drinking hole at the corner of 5th street the Top Hat has a long history of helping cops drink themselves into an early grave along with Manny the owner who as long as I can remember has had that stutter, Hey Manny how's it going,oh usual waiting on my daily drunkard cops who usually come in on a daily, Fuck you Manny give me a drink so I can forget about you and this lousy city.

Detective get your ass off the floor, Macfaras could remember Manny refilling his drink only the last time and then coming out of a blur with this stuttering motherfucker try to say something that sounded like the fifty four Chevy his father had problems starting, time to go home iiimmm putttt uu in a cab…

Sunday 10:34 AM, 214 West College St Philly PA

Sandra Miller knew that there was nothing she could do to help her son, after the Army and the loss of his family he was never the same. She prayed daily by some miracle that he would come back from drugs and the need to live on the streets, he doesn't do well inside of places, it's like he is being chased or need space to run to get away from the demons inside his head.

I heard him on the back porch this morning, I always hear when he makes it home only to stay outside in back in some ways, I feel comfort because on those nights at least I know he is safe. I won't bother him because he will just stay there as if he is hiding and being secretive ….

Nobody

I can see everything from here, and there go that dog Moma say they sold her puppies and she been mad ever since help, help, stop this crazy ass dog, stop I'm fuck you up.....that dog got Tina and Russel scared, Russel on the car talking about that dog know who to fuck with Russel a little sweet he got the stick trying to fight of the dog and he done gave it to Tina and jumped on the car saying girl I'm not made like that and Tina down their like a man and then that dam dog just turned around and left,and they say I'm crazy the things I see make me wonder I come over and sit on Moma back porch and sometimes I remember the old days before they came before they started talking to me every day they use to come sometimes now they just stay, but I remember sometime how it used to be as if I was a spectator in my own life, I remember sometime, I remember warmth and laughter, I remember, I remember ... tic toc tic toc, we here, we here, we your friends, we your friends.

Nobody. December 14, 1989

Chest on fire as if hell was inside trying get out can't see anything where the children or my wife, I must get upstairs can't breathe can't see got to find them fire every were let them be okay, got to get upstairs I see them honey its ok I'm coming I'm coming.

The crash coming down from the ceiling and seeing the fear and dread in the eyes of his wife and child was the last thing David Miller saw as the house caved in from the burning inferno that the fire was.

2:34 AM Philadelphia fire department received a call of a 4-alarm fire on Pratt St in North Philly after the fire was extinguished there was one survivor and two deceased mother and child died from smoke and Burning within the fire the other victim presumed to be the father suffered from third degree burns and smoke inhalation and if he survived his disfigurement it wouldn't be his worst scars.

All David Miller could do was lay on the gurney strapped down as the ambulance with its sirens breaking the quiet of the morning rolling at high speeds in and out of traffic and all David miller could think of was how could life be over and all he felt was pain, pain beyond the ones he had suffered in the fire but pain that could never stop even if he were not dead only the dead could feel this away.

Kick the oxygen up he's going into shock he's convulsing 75 milligrams of benzodiazepine hurry up we are losing him get the boards, clear, clear ....

Nobody.

Beep, Beep, David Miller could vaguely see threw the bandages and with the pain in his head as the light pierced his brain bringing him back to a reality he was not ready to face could not face and just as fast as the pain came the medication filled threw his body as a consolation to his reality and even in his quilt it made him feel everything was ok as he slipped back into darkness of a drug induced sleep.

Paulie Macgregor,

Fish Town was a part of Philadelphia founded in the 1700 later it was predominately inhabited by Irish immigrants a part of the city coming off the Betsy Ross Bridge which separated New Jersey and Pennsylvania once bustling with family and commerce, now as of late we see this area is where the fentanyl aka zombie drug has had its devastating affect which brings us to Paulie MacGregor a product of Fish Town and the ills of modern Fish Town.

Paulie Macgregor fancied himself different that the average junkie because he lavages in the illusion of the past glory of the history of coming from a good family in this area.

They say that a ripple in the water on one side of the world has an affect all the way on the other side also its the reaction of cause and affect it can also be the cautionary tale two boats passing in the night that somehow end up docking at the same island Thus is the case of David Miller aka Nobody and Paulie Mcgregor.

On this day their paths would cross setting into motion events that would change the lives of many, sitting on the stoop David Miller aka Nobody, wasn't having a good day as he had not made any money sitting here panhandling at the bodega on this beautiful day early before the worst of everyone came out.

He wondered what they would tell me today inside his head was a world of its own and he knew in his moments of clarity that something was not right with him, but no one cares so he must go on because the voices loved him made him powerful confident even in his condition of destitution, Hey Hey you, what this crazy white boy want I see him all the time up and down the Ave but we never talked now I wonder what is up.

Hey, you can't make any money down here these people and got shit you need to go uptown with me to the rich side of Philly they give just in hopes of you leaving.

Paulie Macgregor thought when he got close enough to see David Millers face was disfigured and to tell the truth Paulie thought people would give all he wanted with a face like that.

Rittenhouse Square Schuylkill River Park

Amy and Seth Cohen lived in Rittenhouse square a well to do part of the city but on some nights, they would come to the Schuylkill

River Park and camp by the water. Amy thought it was so romantic and something about the night air made their love making so erotic and intense and the restful sleep after.

Amy awaken by the urge hurried out of the tent making sure not to wake Seth as she had to pee and the urge was so great as she made way to a tree near the river the stars were warm for winter making this night more magical and exciting. As she walked, she found comfort and joy and peace finding her place nothing could prepare her for the hands that came from nowhere covering her mouth stopping all effort to make a sound. The more she tried to struggle, the hands became stronger as if they had super human strengthen pushing her forward face down into the grass as if the earth itself knew that this was her final place. As the hand pressed her face harder to the earth, she felt the metal first prick the skin on the back of her neck then deeper into her skull at the base of the neck and all pain was gone then there was nothing but darkness no fear, no pain just endlessness.

Nobody

David Miller and Paulie came up town to panhandle and Paulie was right these rich people give and judge at the same time I could feel the giving in hopes that I would go away and not litter their beautiful streets with my presence, I can feel their eyes on me seeing me and not at the same time as if I am nobody, nothing, look at them all safe and secure looking at all the world as nothing but themselves as important, they are ugly, they are ugly demons, demons in my head they tell me what I must do destroy to bring the light, destroy to bring the light....

Schuylkill River Park 7:45.AM

Dr John Thompson had been with the Philadelphia coroners of for as long as he could remember, and the city has went to hell and a hand basket last week. The victim was a beautiful young woman who had no reason to die as she had and now as he checks this victim, he realized that there is a storm coming, one that most cities and the police really don't like each victim had a small puncture at the nape of the neck same MO yet as of now he didn't want to cause a panic but if he was right which most time he is I would say we have a killer on our hands and he has just got started ....

Detective Macfaras and Davis made their way to this new victim lying face down at the river's edge and her lower clothing halfway down as if she was about to relive herself, we were invited to the district because the coroner thought the cases were related so Davis and Macfaras came and after examining the victim it was unofficially decided that there was the possibility that it could be related.

Paulie hadn't seen David since yesterday after a great day of panhandling in chestnut hills they had caught the 1 back to Fish Town and found the best fix they could find but after David got high, he became strange talking to himself like in another world blowing my buzz and Davis had left unnoticed and that was the last he had saw him.

Detective Davis thought as the evidence was collected that at each crime scene there was this little sliver of silver package that he had seen all over north Philly it was the paper of a popular cheap cigarette the junkies used so they could smoke and use most of their money to get a fix he had ran that thought buy Macfaras but was shut down because they didn't think he had the right to have an opinion but I'm still going to work on my theory because I'm sure that theses killings going to continue.

David Miller was tired he made his way from the shelter on Broad street where they give the homeless showers and a free meal now he was back at his camp under the 1 in a wooded area away from the street just enough so you can sleep without someone walking over you. Davis had him a little tent just like a lot of the homeless in camps all over Philly and most major cities,he was tired he had went back to Chestnut Hill after he and Paulie had come back, he went back because as he was sitting on the street panhandling there was this girl who looked at him and he could see she needed the light and to be free because she was a prisoner of herself and the voices had said that she would see the light and that it was his responsibility to see her find it.

He watched her and her friend camp just as he did and he wondered were they homeless too, but it would change nothing he had to watch and wait down by the rive until the time was right and just when he was there for hours she came out to pee and that was his chance and as she stopped struggling he could see her seem to float into this light right next to the trees that was his acknowledgement that what he was doing was right and for the right reason.

I could feel her relief as I pushed my ice pick as deep and hard as I could through the back of her head, I felt the power the surge goes through my body as the light appeared it was pure ecstasy and in those moments I am whole and I have my family and everything is ok there is no pain no nightmares no burns on my body but there is my child my wife my life.

Detective Macfaras 8:00 AM

Macfaras wishing his head would feel better struggle out of bed looking for his worn coffee pot in hopes if he got coffee somehow, he could find part of his former self or at least enough to where he could function at work.

This case is real, and I will go through the motions I'm not what I used to be the coroner talking this serial killer possibility was something I wasn't ready for, and this call this morning of another possible victim the kid Davis already at the scene waiting for me.

God I never thought that I could drink too much but this morning I feel like shit probably looking the part also in any event must go out and try to find the scum bag responsible. this case has me shook and I wonder how it ends we ran the background on the victims they about as clean as it gets nothing to connects them in a way that would give any profile that would make me think that they would deal with people that would make an unhealthy situation.

One thing all the victims so far have in common is they are dead and no physical evidence except prick at the base of the neck and this small piece of sliver wrapper seeming to be from some type of cigarette,

Maybe today is the day we get a lucky break?

8:45 AM As Davis walked to the crime scene the duty sergeant named Dettori smirked and made a smart remark about has Macfaras finally fell into a bottle he can't get out? Fuck you Sarge Davis said as he approached the area where the victim was laying out on the ground just out of sight from the walkway the first thing that caught Davis eyes was the little sparkle of silver in the grass next to the victim and it occurred to Davis all over North Philly you could see these same tiny pieces of paper especially near the bodegas in the neighborhoods

And it occurred to Davis also that the standard profile may not apply in this case, but he had ran the idea by Macfaras and he had brushed it off as if serial killing were racially biased in the sense that it has to be a certain type or economically viable type of perpetrator times have changed and so have people in this world as of now I think people all people are capable of many heinous acts.

The victim seems to have put up a good struggle unlike the first victim killed on the train it seems he like to come from behind and force the victim face down then making the kill, there is never and assault sexual or otherwise it seems he kills for the sheer sport or joy of it, we have a real sick puppy on our hands.

Putting on glove as not to contaminate evidence, Davis observed that she was about early twenties and that she was not what you would call a beauty by any standards of the word. She was by all definitions butt ugly and as usual like the other victims, he noticed the same wound at the base of the neck and a tiny trickle of blood at the corner of the mouth, her eyes were open as if she could see and speak as if to say see what he did to me? As if somehow her last testimony was to show that she didn't deserve this brutality.

10:13 AM

Macfaras arrived at the scene not looking much better than last night's drunken state yet he knew deep down and so did all the other cops who snickered behind his back that this case and him were a fit because he had overcome one case of this type but also it was the thing that sent his drinking spiraling out of control because he couldn't shake the memories of that case and the sleepless nights and eventually the bottle became his only friend his comforter his solace.

As Macfaras approached the scene, the coroner had arrived along with Davis, he wondered about the kid sometimes he even reminded him of himself at that age young full of fire and hope feeling like having faith in humanity would pay off in the long run but, after years of seeing what they do to each other, those ideas and hope would fade away poor kid, as Macfaras saw the victim he didn't wait he went straight to the victims neck hoping somehow this third victim wouldn't be the same but as he looked he knew that Philly was in for a storm as they all had the same kill injury.

The coroner after his examination came to Davis and Macfaras and gave them his blunt report and told them that this kill was different and that he seems to be on some conquest, and that he seems from past examination of his victims to no so much getting better but not even caring or not having a thought of killing as if he feels spiritually protected which means we have the worst kind of serial killer and yes I said it, it's just one killer in all of the victims.

12:35 PM

Back at command called the round house because of its design and the twenty-four hour court system where perpetrators are processed continually.

The commander along with Macfaras and Davis was giving everyone the riot act stating his expectations of each officer in the apprehension of a suspect and that this case and that yes, we have a serial killer which at this time that information should be kept away from the media at this time until we have information of a public nature.

David Miller felt wonderful today as he walked down Girard St, the sun was shining and he had just come from the mission where they serve meals and had had the meat loaf and given personal hygiene stuff, things like soap toothpaste and on those days were good for people who were less fortunate and somehow those things gave a feeling of normality because a large number of people we find in this condition of not having housing has a lot to do with mental health issues also substance abuse and David Miller fit most categories along with trauma at the loss of his family. But on this day as he walked the Ave, he felt complete with no voices in his head and somehow without them he felt alone abandoned as if some part of him he had lost like the death of an old friend.

But he remembered them each one as they tried to scream and their last fighting breath a last ditch effort at living without a hope of success he had come to the conclusion that the voices were from God and he was chosen to gather those he chose to bring them to the light. He was the one he knew out of all the people in this world he was the one the savior the hand of god as we know him and he was ready to do as a god has commanded.

Slipping off the Ave into an abandoned house David Miller had to have his fix as he tied off the vain he realized that what he was about to do was soar to some unknown place with his God his savior and as the substance entered his blood stream all that mattered became part of the darkness as David Miller drifted into what they call on the street the junkie nod.....

After leaving command Macfaras and Davis made their way to Geno's a popular pizza spot in west Philly known for great cheese steaks not that they had an appetite after the lecture from command they made their way back to a booth overlooking south St and the silence between them was thick knowing after the briefing that the next victim was on the way.

Sitting at the table with all the case files both understood they had nothing Macfaras told Davis that they need to hit the street and follow every idea no matter how farfetched at that moment Davis up and left as if he had seen a ghost telling Macfaras he would call him within an hour.

Day before yesterday Davis had remembered on his off day he was going into the bodega on Grit St in north Philly where he use to go as a kid to buy tamales, but the incident was brief he had almost been run over by this homeless guy with his face covered and he could tell his face had been injured but as the two passed the homeless dude they bumped each other and out of his pocket fell to the ground a package of cheap cigarettes with the silver wrapper.

After hours of sitting in the car along the street where the incident occurred Davis knew that his chances were slim that he would encounter the same person, but he also knew that the homeless drug addicted people were in a sense migratory in their habits of convenience so the likelihood was 50 50 that this guy would magically appear, it was a long shot.

Davis reflected as he sat there in the neighborhood in the street how much the area had changed as he remembered families and children playing in the street that was then, people with children with any sense kept their kids inside for safety because on every street corner there is open area drug sales and the used needles of the junkies litter the streets as if its normal for people to just discard not caring for life of others nor having a sense of Community.

Davis reflected on his mother working all her life to pay for her home only for it to be worthless because of the ills of a nation that imprisons it's citizens for drug use yet there are no Poppie fields nor cocaine planting on the continent yet in those places the people frown upon its use, figure that.

Detective Davis

After a long day of nothing he decided to return to the first crime scene at Septa Transportation to check out surveillance video tapes from the first victim he met, Stanly Burks third generation station master as he led Davis to the viewing room Davis noticed that the electronics had seen its better days but hopefully the recording could shed some light on the murder.

As he watched the tapes he saw the first victim board the train and right after he saw a figure face covered but grainy quality of the tapes made it hard to identify but there was something familiar about his presence as he boarded right behind our victim but that's where the video loses focus and then picks up with our stranger leaving before our victim was found, yes he is our guy but who he is, is a mystery.

He decided it was time to catch up with his partner, and they decided to meet at the Top Hat Bar at 630 to discuss their findings from the day's exploits.

Macfaras arrived at the location before Davis arrived, he was at his usual place drinking bourbon neat already well into his second drink as Davis arrived, he was feeling no pain and things seemed to not be so heavy on his mind, hey kid have a seat, let's talk shop I have the toxicology reports on all our victim seems they have something in common with the party favorite, they all had traces of fentanyl and heroin in their system, Davis chimes in what do you think about my thoughts about them knowing the same person from that part of town where most of this junk is sold? Macfaras had to consider every possibility, but he couldn't rap his mind that these sheltered pure bread little simps would even have the balls to venture in that part of

Philly let alone to cope dope. No, they had someone help them and that's our common denominator.

Davis looked at the tapes and that he had a hunch about the guy on the tape, but Macfaras saw him and felt he was just some homeless bum out of place at the wrong place just there at the wrong time after all no one witnesses the actual murder only him leaving the train, but Davis felt deep in his gut he was right.

After their brainstorming, Davis and Macfaras had drinks and began to know each other as people and one thing Davis realized is that Macfaras could drink with the best of them after a few drinks Davis took his leave with much on his mind and with a new determination he felt he himself was on the right track if no one else believed, he was sure.

Nobody

Meanwhile David Miller had got off the train and made his way to Rittenhouse square working his way back to the corner were the Italian bakery was. He liked it there the people seem to give better as he sits their looking just as he was a panhandler or so they thought but he knew better he knew he was much more he was the hand of God here as if he was just a nobody and that thought made him feel that he had fooled the world look at them walking by some with contempt and others with their fake concerns if they only knew he was the one.

Sonny George had lived in Rittenhouse square most of his life he had seen changes in his community over the years some for the better and some he did not like, he had seen the homeless migrate to the community to beg for money on the streets and he understood that more than most though he had never seen poverty in his life he longed to find the answer to the problem because no one should go hungry are be living on the street. See, he believed that the greed of America was real and that it was up to people like himself to make America live up to its promises.

Sonny George was one of those liberal millennials born at a time when the nation was suffering growing pains and the new idealismwhich was deterred by hate religion that was not of this nation nor any but a fallacy part truth and lies that were not of European origin but forced upon this nation and throughout the world and it was those whom held these ideals held our nation in a choke hold along with that of the one percent of the population which held all the wealth getting more rich as they create issues to divide the mass's to keep them from really coming together and seeing what they are really doing this was the mind of Sonny George and today he was going to make a difference he was going out on the streets and be on the front line uplifting those anywhere he happen to find them today it was that day.

Sandra Miller

Today was a beautiful Sunday at church and after a beautiful dinner and as she relished the day her mind wondered of her son how was he? Was he hungry or cold on these mean streets or was he in pain and in need as she thought she felt more helpless but one thing she had was the memories and how proud she was of her boy after he got into the military top of his class and sent straight to Iraq and Afghanistan one place after another he was gone for years and after he came home on leave she was none the less proud but he was not her boy anymore it seemed his eyes were looking at things he had seen and done as if they were forever in the front of his thoughts and mind.

Yes, he was home but not the same and Kelsie was a nice girl they had gotten married after he got home, and they were a beautiful family and the day he lost them in the fire he was lost also his mind seemed to just blank out he could never stand to be inside or even sleep we had taken him to the VA and they gave him all these drugs and it worked for a while but eventually he just wandered off for days at a time and as long as he didn't hurt anyone there was nothing the authorities could do shameful all he gave for this country they just forgot about him.

Sandra Miller was resolved that her son was in God's hands and that whatever happened it would be God's will...

Detective Macfaras made it home from the Top Hat bar none too good as he was as drunk as he ever had been, but it seemed he was in the state of mind to think about the case at present he often thought about all the evidence and came to the best-case scenario he had been informed that from command the previous day that a special agent from the local FBI office was coming by to assist our local cops as though we were incompetent, Macfaras resented the implication's but he had no choice but to apply, this agent was some hot shot profiler which was even more room for resentments.

Nobody

David Miller awakes from a drug filled night, all alone, no voices and all the reality he had felt in years came rushing back. All the clouded thoughts and memories which had faded came rushing in causing a panic of emotions as if he had been sleep in a nightmare that was his life his wife and child's death and the murders he had done at the assisting of the God in his mind here he was standing in this cold with bloodied hands, crying as he had never done as the cold December wind blew at his old tattered unwashed coat all he could do was run as if he was being chased by shame and all the pain of loss that he had forgotten because of trauma as he ran through the ice covered streets of Kensington looking to hide and to find some place to be alone.

Nobody

As David Miller ran, he decided to go to the homeless camp near the old shipping yard. He ran on past the camp to the old abandoned train station up high above the camp and found an abandoned truck decaying in the last place it was parked.

Nobody

David Miller had decided to stay here away from everyone thinking that the God in his head was no God but the devil and he had chosen him as the weapon to deliver his vengeance and he remembered the smells the taste of blood in his nostrils and its smell like the spirit of each victim lingering with him after each deed done, but now there were no voices only the musk of an aging truck and the flicker of candles he had bought earlier now using them for light and warmth, he had decided he would just hide until his God or his Devil would tell him what to do.

8:00 AM

Davis and Macfaras sit in the conference room across for the agent that was sent to give profile of their suspect and as they sit there across from this well dressed manicured nailed college boy, he begins to give the general stagnant description of a suspect and Macfaras decided that it was a waste of time and left the conference no better off than before.

Davis and Macfaras decided to wait and go back to each crime scene to see if any witness could be up and down Chestnut Hill they inquired about usual people that some of the business owners may have seen and as the day went by it was evident that these people had the attention span of three year olds only interested in their own wellbeing as if only they excised in this realm of reality. Things were going just like this until they came to an Italian bakery on spring street where there was this young man sitting on the stoop playing an indescribable instrument. And he was a sight for sore eyes with his red dread locks and beads just sitting there as piece some bohemian artwork on full display one could venture to say that in some way, he was majestic in the out of place sort of way.

This young man after further questing was Sonny George just another fixture of the landscape of the privileged and illusioned or delusional population of the city these people feel as if money should protect them from the reality of the ugliness that most of the world is affected by being in law enforcement most cops know that the nature of people are the same with or without economical securities there are stores after stories of the carnage people do in both sectors.

Sonny George

What else you want the man the all-seeing eyes of our oppressed nation nothing down here except brothers in need those who live to survive on a daily man!!!!!

Macfaras was feed up, knock off the bullshit you little want to be motherfucker look at you on some revolution of your own guilt you lil maggot have a good day...

Davis and Macfaras after leaving Chestnut Hill were riding in silence wondering if their man would strike again and where it had occurred to them that most of the victims were all from the same area except the one from the train but she also was a resident of Chestnut Hill so they felt they would form their own small task force of volunteers to do each area at night to see what they could find.

Nobody

They are there waiting to be healed to be saved, waking up head on fire words so many words all at the same time David Miller was in his madness not knowing how long nor what time it was,but he did know that it was time to go out and do his Gods work no matter what it had to be it must be because his voices were more clarified as ever before as if he and God were one he glowed as he looked at his hands like magic or madness either way he had power as never before and all he could do was move.

Nobody, 9:42 PM .

David Miller had made his way to Rittenhouse Park in Chestnut Hill and felt odd because he saw this poinsettia plant as big as a tree with its red berries and pin prick leaves and somehow he needed to be near it in it he climbed in not even caring about the picks he felt on his way up to the place he could just sit and wait for a word a sign for what must be done next and sitting there a song he heard as sweet as angels as if it were a heaven this must be what it sounds like and it comforted him as he just sat there .

As David Miller sat there, he heard a voice and this unusual music and someone approaching down below under his tree, he looked down and knew without hesitation that his God had sent this person to be released to be brought into the light and just at that moment he took his right hand and found his ice pick stuck in one side of his worn boot and braced himself as he jumped with all the strength and rage that he had. He came down with all his force and could feel the cold steel hit the base of the neck hard and the young man let out a scream but did not fall but instead jumped around as David held on with all his strength grabbing him by the mouth as he bit down on his hand but he felt no pain only determination to do as his God had commanded.

10:00 PM

Detective Davis heard the sound of a scream down by the river in the park and took to a full trot with Macfaras far behind him at some distance as Davis held his flashlight and weapon, he saw two figures one holding on from the back as the other screamed in pain. Davis knew it was the homeless man from the tapes he screamed police and getting a clear shot discharging two shots seeming to hit its mark as the assailant fell into the river going straight to the bottom as the surface water churned violently into the darkness.

Davis and Macfaras kneeling over the victim they knew that he was dead also that it was the young man earlier from the bakery it was Sonny George, the one who wanted to be revolutionist.

Nobody

David Miller felt the cold water and a burn and a feeling of peace he had not felt in years as the cold river wrapped him on all sides this cold peaceful warmth and there were no voices only peace, peace like never before his God had taken him.

Seemed like the whole of the Philadelphia police force had come out to this spot of the last victim, and the assailant seemed to have been taken by the police and the news and the bad weather pushing in from Canada had made its way also to the crime scene it was a buzz as the cleat mixed with rain and snow came as if to signify that some victory had be accomplished as the crime scene went on despite the angry weather that seemed to be befitting of the occasion.

Nobody

Cold so cold shivering somehow the current had swiftly carried David Miller to the Jersey side of the river as he washed up on the shore, he could only hear the voice that said not yet,not yet sleep, sleep you must rest the book of never ending the book of retribution is yet to come...

They say that we sometimes die yet we live on as this entity that exists to remind the living to appreciate each day as if tomorrow does not have to come and, in that way, we each live for a purpose other than our own self-interest other than making our pleasure our only reason for being and somehow we know then that tomorrow may just not come...

www.ingramcontent.com/pod-product-compliance
Lightning Source LLC
Chambersburg PA
CBHW022054170626
46808CB00003B/1470